*To my beloved "Señorita Swing"*
*(a.k.a. Carol Morrissey Greiner)*
*—T. deP.*

*For Michael Frith,*
*artist, mentor, friend*
*—J. L.*

SIMON & SCHUSTER BOOKS FOR YOUNG READERS
An imprint of Simon & Schuster Children's Publishing Division
1230 Avenue of the Americas, New York, New York 10020
Text copyright © 2017 by Tomie dePaola and Jim Lewis
Illustrations copyright © 2017 by Tomie dePaola
SIMON & SCHUSTER BOOKS FOR YOUNG READERS is a trademark
of Simon & Schuster, Inc.
For information about special discounts for bulk purchases, please contact Simon & Schuster
Special Sales at 1-866-506-1949 or business@simonandschuster.com.
The Simon & Schuster Speakers Bureau can bring authors to your live event.
For more information or to book an event, contact the Simon & Schuster Speakers Bureau
at 1-866-248-3049 or visit our website at www.simonspeakers.com.
Book design by Laurent Linn
The text for this book was set in Minister Std.
The illustrations for this book were rendered in acrylics with colored pencil
on 150lb Fabriano Cold Press 100% rag watercolor paper.
Manufactured in China
0317 SCP
First Edition
2 4 6 8 10 9 7 5 3 1
CIP data for this book is available from the Library of Congress.
ISBN 978-1-4814-7947-9
ISBN 978-1-4814-7948-6 (eBook)

# Andy & Sandy
## and the
# Big Talent Show

## Tomie dePaola
### COWRITTEN WITH Jim Lewis

SIMON & SCHUSTER BOOKS FOR YOUNG READERS
New York   London   Toronto   Sydney   New Delhi

We should enter!

# What's my talent?

Can you
juggle?

Can you
tumble?

# Can you hula hoop?

I cannot do that

or that

or that.

We can do a dance—
together!

I cannot do that, either!

It is easy.
Follow me.

You just have to practice.

*And now . . .*

ANDY
AND
SANDY
SASHAY
THROUGH
THE
PARK

*Psst*, Sandy.
Follow me.

# The winners!

Now we take a bow—

together.

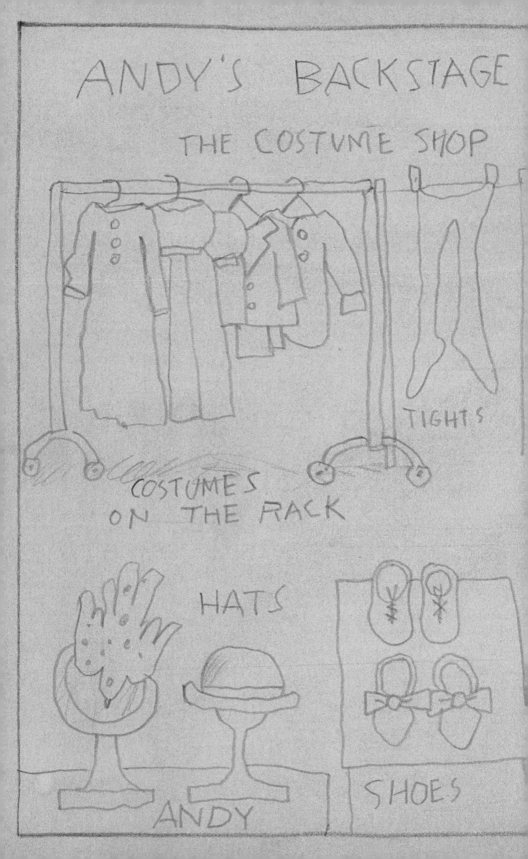